DATE DUE

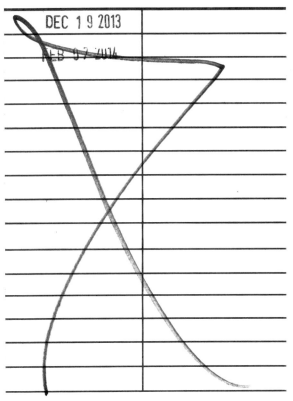

BRODART, CO. Cat. No. 23-221-003

Promontory Heights Elementary
46200 Stoneview Dr
Chilliwack, BC V2R 5W8

Natural Disasters

Blizzards

by
Jean Allen

Consultant:
Stephen J. Colucci
Professor of Atmospheric Sciences
Cornell University

CAPSTONE
HIGH-INTEREST
BOOKS

an imprint of Capstone Press
Mankato, Minnesota

Capstone High-Interest Books are published by Capstone Press
151 Good Counsel Drive, P.O. Box 669, Mankato, Minnesota 56002
http://www.capstonepress.com

Copyright © 2003 Capstone Press. All rights reserved.
No part of this book may be reproduced without written permission from the publisher.
The publisher takes no responsibility for the use of any of the materials or methods
described in this book, nor for the products thereof.
Printed in the United States of America

Library of Congress Cataloging-in-Publication Data
Allen, Jean, 1964–
Blizzards/by Jean Allen.
　　p.cm.—(Natural disasters)
　　Includes bibliographical references and index.
　　ISBN 0-7368-3466-4 (paperback)　ISBN 0-7368-0899-X (hardcover)
　　1. Blizzards—Juvenile literature. [1. Blizzards.] I. Title. II. Natural disasters
(Capstone Press)
QC926.37 .A55 2002
551.55'5—dc21　　　　　　　　　　　　　　　　　　　00-013195

Summary: Describes how and why blizzards form, the damage they cause, ways to
predict them, and some of the most disastrous blizzards of the past.

Editorial Credits
Gillia M. Olson, editor; Lois Wallentine, product planning editor;
　　Timothy Halldin, cover designer and illustrator; Katy Kudela, photo researcher

Photo Credits
Bettmann/CORBIS, 28
Frank Cezus/FPG International LLC, 36
Frank Grant/International Stock, 10
Jeff Henry/Roche Jaune Pictures, Inc., 26, 43
Jim Baron/The Image Finders, 12
Kent and Donna Dannen, 18
Larry Prosor, cover, 24, 38
Martha Cooper/The Viesti Collection, Inc., 8
Minneapolis Star Journal/Minnesota Historical Society, 6
Minnesota Historical Society, 4
Photri-Microstock/Steve Lissau, 16
Reuters/Mike Segar/Archive Photos, 30; Reuters/Archive Photos, 32;
　　Reuters/Mark Caldwell/Archive Photos, 34
Unicorn Stock Photos/Marie Mills, 41
Visuals Unlimited, 22

1　2　3　4　5　6　08　07　06　05　04　03

Table of Contents

Chapter 1	Blizzards	5
Chapter 2	Why Blizzards Happen	11
Chapter 3	The Power of a Blizzard	19
Chapter 4	Famous Blizzards	29
Chapter 5	Surviving a Blizzard	37

Map 15

Words to Know 44

To Learn More 45

Useful Addresses 46

Internet Sites 47

Index 48

Chapter 1

Blizzards

Armistice Day on November 11, 1940, started out as a warm fall day. Armistice Day celebrated the end of World War I. It is now known as Veterans Day. It honors veterans of all wars. Temperatures were above 60 degrees Fahrenheit (16 degrees Celsius). But by noon, snow was thick in the air in Sauk Rapids, Minnesota. The wind was blowing fiercely when Joanne Carlin boarded the bus after school.

The bus driver could barely see the road. The wind was blowing the snow all around. The driver watched telephone poles along the road to try to guide the bus. But the driver could not see clearly through the thick snow. The bus went into a ditch. Joanne and about 12 other students waited in the bus. The driver went for help.

The Armistice Day Blizzard forced people to dig through huge snow drifts.

5

Many cars were stuck in deep snow during the Armistice Day Blizzard.

A nearby farmer suggested that the driver take the students to a small grocery store. It was one-fourth of a mile (.4 kilometer) away. The bus driver and students tramped through the snow. They held hands to make sure no one would get lost.

At the store, the students stood around a wood stove to warm themselves. The store's owners gave them food and blankets. The students worried about their families. They could not contact anyone. Telephone lines were down. All they could do was wait.

The students played cards to pass the time. The boys took turns shoveling a path to the outdoor toilet. The path seemed to fill with snow almost as fast as they cleared it.

Two days later, the county snowplow finally passed by the store. Joanne's father came behind it to take her home. Joanne and her family were safe. Others were not so lucky.

The Armistice Day Blizzard blasted the Midwest and Great Lakes region for 60 hours. The wind whipped up to 2 feet (.6 meter) of snow into high, hard drifts. The drifts blocked roads and nearly buried buildings.

Many people were unprepared for the cold weather. They left home in the morning with only light coats and no hats, scarves, or boots.

The blizzard claimed lives in a number of ways. Some people became lost in the blinding snow and froze to death. Others froze to death while they were stranded in their cars. On Lake Michigan, 69 people died when ships sank. Altogether, 154 people died in the Armistice Day Blizzard.

▶ **High winds can form drifts that cover cars.**

Blizzards

A blizzard is a winter storm that includes both snow and wind. Blizzards have winds of at least 35 miles (56 kilometers) per hour. Blizzards' falling or blowing snow reduces visibility to one-fourth mile (.4 kilometer) or less for at least three hours.

A severe blizzard has winds of more than 45 miles (72 kilometers) per hour and near zero visibility. Severe blizzards also must have temperatures less than 10 degrees Fahrenheit (–12 degrees Celsius).

In the United States, blizzards are most common in the north central and northeastern areas. They also are common in Canada, the former Soviet Union, and the polar regions. Blizzards are most likely to take place during December, January, and February in the Northern Hemisphere. This area is located above the equator. The equator is an imaginary line that extends around Earth's middle. Each year, between one and seven blizzards occur in North America.

A blizzard can bring an entire region to a standstill. Snowdrifts block roads. Wind may knock down trees and power lines and damage houses. People often are left without heat, electricity, or telephone service for several days. In the mountains, blizzards can cause snow, rocks, and ice to suddenly break off and fall down. These avalanches can bury people and houses. On oceans or large lakes, blizzards can cause large waves that can sink ships.

Chapter 2

Why Blizzards Happen

Blizzards are severe weather events. They are caused by changes in air pressure, temperature, and moisture.

The Atmosphere

The atmosphere is the layer of air that surrounds Earth. Air has weight. Air pressure describes this weight on a surface.

Temperature changes the air's weight. Air expands when it is heated. Warm air becomes lighter and rises. Cooler, heavier air flows in to take its place. This moving air is called wind. Wind always is caused by changes in air pressure.

Wind is caused by changes in air pressure.

➢ **Large flakes form when the air is very moist.**

Temperature also affects the amount of moisture air can hold. Warm air can hold more moisture than cool air. Clouds form when tiny droplets of water join together to form bigger drops. This process is condensation. The drops fall as rain once they become too heavy.

How Snow Forms
Water droplets turn into ice crystals when the air temperature falls below freezing. Water

freezes at 32 degrees Fahrenheit (0 degrees Celsius). These ice crystals join together and form snowflakes. The amount of moisture in the air determines the size of the snowflakes. Large flakes develop in moist conditions. Small flakes develop in dry conditions.

How Blizzards Form

Air masses are responsible for weather. These large bodies of air have about the same amount of moisture throughout. They can cover hundreds of miles. Air masses are constantly moving throughout the world. Cold polar air masses form near the North and South poles. Warm air masses form near the equator.

The edge between warm and cold air masses is called a front. Storms can occur along fronts. Storms spin counterclockwise in the Northern Hemisphere. This spinning brings cold air to the south and warm air to the north. Wind is produced. The cold air is heavier and stays closer to the ground. The warm air rises above the cold air. But the warm air cools off as it rises. The moisture in the rising warm air becomes rain or snow.

Jet streams also help form blizzards. These strong, stable air currents usually are located 5 to 7 miles (8 to 11 kilometers) above Earth's surface. Blizzards can form when a jet stream bulges south during the winter. This bulge allows cold polar air to go south. At the same time, warm tropical air flows north. Snowstorms are likely to occur if the polar and tropical air masses meet.

Regional Storms

Certain storm patterns often form in particular regions. North America's East Coast experiences nor'easters. These winter storms have strong winds that blow in from the Atlantic Ocean. Nor'easters can form in an area from the U.S. state of Virginia to Newfoundland, Canada. Nor'easters produce heavy snow or rain and high ocean waves.

In other areas, winter storms can result from the lake effect. The largest lakes usually do not freeze in the winter. The lakes' water

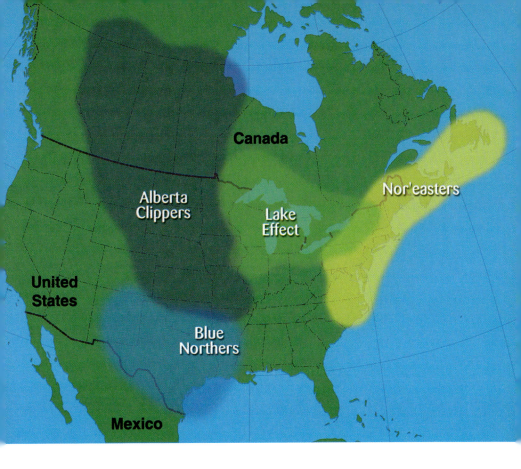

temperatures can be much warmer than the surrounding air. Tiny water droplets rise into the warm air above the lakes. Wind carries this water vapor toward land. The moist air cools over land. This process can produce large amounts of snow.

The Great Lakes region experiences many winter storms due to the lake effect. In the United States, this area extends from

Minnesota to Maine. The area also includes southern Ontario and southern Quebec, Canada. This area of North America sometimes is called the Snowbelt.

In Canada, many blizzards develop east of the Rocky Mountains over the province of Alberta. These blizzards are called Alberta Clippers. These storms move in a southeasterly direction toward Manitoba and North Dakota.

Alberta Clippers usually last less than 12 hours. But the wind speeds can be very high. In March 1941, an Alberta Clipper produced winds higher than 62 miles (100 kilometers) per hour. This storm caused 76 deaths in southern Canada and the northern United States.

Alberta Clippers sometimes reach as far south as Texas. The cold air meets the warm, moist air from the Gulf of Mexico. This front can produce heavy snowfall. These storms are called Blue Northers.

Large lakes often are warmer than the surrounding air.

Chapter 3

The Power of a Blizzard

Blizzards rarely are as damaging as other severe weather events such as tornadoes or hurricanes. But blizzards still are very dangerous. Wind chill is the one of the biggest threats.

Wind Chill
The wind chill is a way of describing how cold air feels to living things. Temperature and wind speed are used to compute the wind chill. A strong wind chill can make temperatures feel much colder than they really are. High wind speed and falling temperatures combine to quickly increase the wind chill.

Wind can make the temperature seem colder.

The Wind Chill Factor

The wind chill factor can vary depending on other conditions. Sunny skies can make the air feel warmer. The amount of wind an area receives also has an effect on the wind chill factor. The wind chill factor is not used for temperatures above 35 degrees Fahrenheit (2 degrees Celsius).

Temperature in Fahrenheit

Wind Speed MPH	35	30	25	20	15	10	5	0	-5	-10	-15	-20	-25	-30
10	22	16	10	3	-3	-9	-15	-22	-27	-34	-40	-46	-52	-58
15	16	9	2	-3	-11	-16	-25	-31	-36	-45	-51	-58	-65	-72
20	12	4	-3	-10	-17	-24	-31	-39	-46	-53	-60	-67	-74	-81
25	8	1	-7	-15	-22	-29	-36	-44	-51	-59	-66	-74	-81	-88
30	6	-2	-10	-18	-25	-33	-41	-49	-56	-64	-71	-79	-86	-93
35	4	-4	-12	-20	-27	-35	-43	-52	-58	-67	-74	-82	-89	-97
40	3	-5	-13	-21	-29	-37	-45	-53	-60	-69	-76	-84	-92	-100

Temperature in Celsius

Wind Speed KPH	2	-1	-4	-7	-9	-12	-15	-18	-21	-23	-26	-29	-32	-34
16	-6	-9	-13	-16	-19	-23	-26	-29	-33	-36	-39	-43	-47	-50
24	-9	-13	-17	-21	-24	-28	-32	-38	-40	-43	-46	-50	-54	-58
32	-11	-16	-20	-23	-27	-32	-36	-39	-43	-47	-51	-55	-60	-63
40	-14	-18	-22	-25	-30	-34	-38	-42	-47	-51	-55	-59	-64	-67
48	-15	-19	-24	-28	-32	-36	-41	-44	-49	-53	-57	-62	-66	-70
56	-16	-20	-25	-29	-33	-37	-42	-45	-51	-55	-58	-63	-68	-72
64	-17	-21	-26	-29	-34	-38	-43	-47	-52	-56	-60	-65	-70	-73

Wind Speed | Temperature | Dangerous | Increasing Danger | Very Dangerous

Wind carries heat away from living things. Wind chill makes body temperatures go down more quickly than if there were no wind. People and other living things have less time outside before their bodies begin to freeze. This cooling effect makes the wind chill very dangerous.

Frostbite and Hypothermia
In severe cold, the body tries to protect its vital inner organs. The body sends more blood to the heart, lungs, liver, and kidneys. Less blood is able to flow to the body's extremities. These body parts include the hands, feet, ears, and nose. The flesh on people's extremities may lose feeling and turn white or pale.

Frostbite occurs when flesh freezes. Frostbite can cause permanent damage. Tissue begins to decay when the blood flow stops. The affected tissue can die. This condition is called gangrene. The dead tissue must be removed. Doctors may have to perform an operation to remove the affected area.

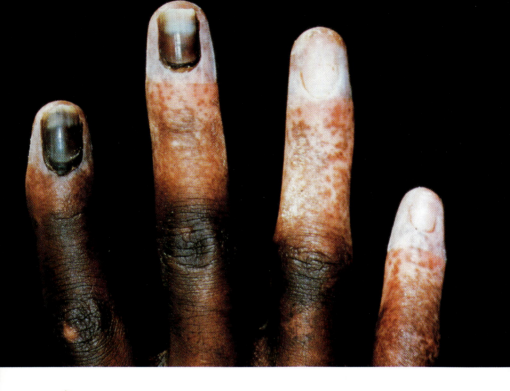

▷ **Flesh turns white during the early stages of frostbite.**

    Hypothermia is another danger of cold weather. Hypothermia occurs when the body's temperature drops to less than 95 degrees Fahrenheit (35 degrees Celsius). Most people's normal body temperature is 98.6 degrees Fahrenheit (37 degrees Celsius). Symptoms of hypothermia include uncontrollable shivering, tiredness, and stumbling. Memory loss and slurred speech also indicate hypothermia. Hypothermia can lead to death.

Both frostbite and hypothermia are serious conditions that require medical care. If medical help is not available, people should slowly warm the victim. They should remove the victim's wet clothing and replace it with dry clothing and blankets. In severe cases, people can use their own body heat to help warm the victim.

Victims of hypothermia must be warmed carefully. The center of the body should be warmed first. Cold blood flows to the heart if the arms or legs are warmed first. This situation can cause heart failure.

Other Dangers

Every year, blizzards, winter storms, and cold temperatures kill about 100 people in the United States. The exact number of deaths is difficult to determine. Many of the deaths are not directly related to the weather. Traffic accidents cause the most deaths. Heart attacks from snow shoveling also lead to many deaths.

Men who are older than 60 have the greatest risk from heart attacks due to snow shoveling.

Avalanches are possible dangers in mountainous areas. An avalanche buries anything in its path. The wall of snow can travel as fast as 240 miles (386 kilometers) per hour.

Predicting Blizzards

Today, scientists use many tools to forecast the weather. Satellites circling Earth take pictures of cloud systems. Doppler radar provides detailed information about rainfall, snowfall, and wind conditions in specific areas. It uses radio signals to create a visual image of weather patterns. Powerful computers help scientists use this information to predict the weather.

Winter storms still can be difficult to predict. Heavy snow sometimes falls in small areas that are too narrow to show up on radar. Temperatures can drop quickly. A few degrees can make the difference between a rainy day and a severe winter storm.

Experts try to control avalanches by purposely causing smaller avalanches.

▷ Blowing snow can cause very deep drifts.

Watches and Warnings

The National Weather Service (NWS) issues watches, warnings, and advisories to keep people aware of winter weather. These notices are broadcast over television, radio, and the Internet. They also are broadcast over a special radio network called NOAA (National Oceanic and Atmospheric Administration) weather radio. Special radios broadcast these messages.

These weather radios can sound an alert if severe weather is expected in a specific area.

The NWS issues different types of watches, warnings, and advisories. It issues a winter storm watch if severe winter weather such as heavy snow is possible in the next day or two.

The NWS also issues winter storm warnings. Warnings mean severe winter weather conditions are occurring or are highly likely to occur. Blizzard warnings mean strong conditions will likely produce low visibility, deep drifts, and life-threatening wind chills.

Advisories also alert people to possible weather problems. Snow advisories mean snowfall of 3 to 5 inches (8 to 13 centimeters) is expected. Blowing and drifting snow advisories mean blowing snow will cause poor visibility and dangerous driving conditions. Wind chill advisories mean wind chills of –20 degrees Fahrenheit (–29 degrees Celsius) or colder are expected.

Chapter 4

Famous Blizzards

Blizzards have caused great damage and loss of life. Studying past blizzards can help people prepare for and prevent problems caused by future blizzards.

The Blizzard of 1888
The Blizzard of 1888 was an especially fierce nor'easter. It blasted the northeastern United States from March 12 to 14. The storm began with heavy rain along the East Coast. The temperature dropped quickly. The rain turned to snow as the wind speed increased.

Official sources say wind speeds reached 48 miles (77 kilometers) per hour. Huge amounts of snow fell. Connecticut and Massachusetts received 50 inches (127 centimeters) of snow.

The Blizzard of 1888 caused telephone and electricity poles to tip.

Giant snowdrifts towered 15 to 50 feet (5 to 15 meters) high. Entire buildings were buried. Snowdrifts even blocked the raised railways of New York City.

Damage from this storm was widespread. Wind and snow snapped telegraph and telephone wires. Communication between cities was impossible. The storm sank or damaged 200 ships along the East Coast. Altogether, about 400 people died in the Blizzard of 1888.

The Storm of the Century
Another large storm happened exactly 105 years after the Blizzard of 1888. It is called the Storm of the Century. From March 12 to 14, 1993, this blizzard dropped heavy snow over 26 states. These states were along the East Coast. Many areas received more than 24 inches (61 centimeters) of snow. The storm also affected Canada and Mexico.

Traffic was almost entirely stopped for three days. All interstate highways north of Atlanta, Georgia, were closed. Every major East Coast

The Storm of the Century dropped heavy snow over 26 states.

airport was closed at some point during the storm.

Different regions experienced the storm in different ways. On Long Island, New York, pounding waves caused 18 homes to fall into the ocean. People reported 65-foot (20-meter) waves off the coast of Nova Scotia, Canada. The storm was powerful enough to sink a 581-foot (177-meter) ship. All 33 members of the crew were killed. Wind gusts as high as 144 miles (232 kilometers) per hour were reported on Mount Logan in New Hampshire.

Blizzards were not the only forms of severe weather that happened during this storm. In Florida, 15 tornadoes killed dozens of people.

By the time it was over, the storm had affected half of the United States' population. Roofs collapsed under snow's weight. Millions of people were without power. An estimated 270 people died. Another 48 people were reported missing at sea.

The Storm of the Century also caused 15 tornadoes in Florida.

The Blizzard of 1996

The Blizzard of 1996 began January 6. It lasted until January 8. The storm affected 22 states along the East Coast. The storm area extended from Georgia to Maine and inland as far west as Indiana. Some major East Coast cities received 20 inches (51 centimeters) of snow or more. Philadelphia, Pennsylvania, received about 31 inches (79 centimeters). The storm's greatest snowfall was in West Virginia. The Snowshoe Ski Resort received 48 inches (122 centimeters) of snow. The resort area also reported wind gusts of more than 50 miles (80 kilometers) per hour.

Damage continued after the storm ended. Sudden warm temperatures caused the snow to melt faster than the ground could absorb it. Heavy rain also occurred. The combination of rain and melting snow led to serious flooding. Some rivers rose as high as 20 feet (6 meters) above their banks. The flooding killed 33 people and left thousands homeless.

The Blizzard of 1996 made deep drifts in many areas of the East Coast.

35

Chapter 5

Surviving a Blizzard

Blizzards cause many deaths each year. But simple planning can reduce the risk of death or injury during a blizzard.

Traveling in a Blizzard
People should avoid any unnecessary travel during a blizzard or winter storm. People should take great care when forced to drive during a storm. They should travel with another person and drive only during daylight hours. They also should keep the vehicle's gas tank full and tell another person about their travel plans.

People should have winter survival kits in their vehicles. The kits should include a first aid kit, extra supplies of medications, a

---

People should avoid unnecessary travel in blizzards because of slippery conditions and poor visibility.

flashlight, a battery-powered radio, and extra batteries. The kit also should include bottled water and high-energy food such as nuts and dried fruit. Warm clothing, blankets, and a bright cloth are good additions to the kit. The cloth can be used as a flag to signal rescuers. People can use a candle and waterproof matches as a heat source. People can melt snow to make drinking water using a small can and the matches.

People also should carry other items in their vehicles. Other useful items include a shovel, tow rope, compass, booster cables, and road maps. Tissues and a large can with a plastic cover also are useful. These items may be necessary to use as a toilet.

Traffic accidents are more likely to occur when people do not completely clear snow and ice from their vehicles. An ice scraper and brush remove snow, frost, and ice from the car. The windshield and all windows should be clear. People should brush off the front and rear lights. Other drivers can see the vehicle more easily when the lights are clear of snow.

People always should be sure that their vehicles are cleared of snow and ice.

Stranded in a Blizzard

People should stay with their vehicle if they are stranded during a blizzard. It is very easy to get confused and lost in blowing snow. Being lost in open country during a blizzard means almost certain death.

In the vehicle, people should stay warm and alert. They should tie a bright cloth to the vehicle's antenna. The driver should run the vehicle's engine for about ten minutes every hour. People should use the heater during this time. The exhaust pipe should be clear of snow. Toxic fumes can back up into the car if the exhaust is not clear. People can crack a window facing away from the wind to let fresh air into the vehicle.

People caught outdoors during a blizzard should try to seek some shelter. They should cover all exposed parts of their bodies. People should move their arms and legs to stay warm. They should wait for the storm to lessen or for help to arrive before leaving the shelter.

People caught outside during a blizzard should seek shelter.

After a Blizzard

Anyone outdoors in the cold should dress properly. Layered clothes trap air between the layers. Trapped air helps the body conserve heat. Hats are very important for conserving body heat. More than half of a person's body heat is lost through the top of the head. People should change out of wet clothes. Clothes lose most of their protective value when they are wet. Frostbite and hypothermia then are more likely to occur.

Snowplows are likely to be out during and after winter storms. Drivers should give them plenty of room to work. Children may enjoy playing in fresh snow after a storm. But they should avoid playing in areas near traffic.

People also need to remove snow where it interferes with daily life. People in towns usually need to shovel their sidewalks. Rock salt can be placed on sidewalks and stairs to melt leftover ice and snow.

Snow can be very heavy. Roofs can cave in from the weight of snow. People can prevent cave-ins by removing large amounts of snow from roofs.

A blizzard represents winter weather at its most extreme. The cold, snow, and wind of a blizzard are a strong reminder of nature's power. But people can prepare for and survive many blizzard conditions.

People should remove heavy snow from roofs.

Words To Know

accumulation (uh-kyoo-myuh-LAY-shun)—
the depth of the snow that is received in a
particular area

air pressure (AIR PRESH-ur)—the weight of
air on a surface

Doppler radar (DOP-ler RAY-dar)—a weather
tool that uses radio signals to create a visual
image of weather patterns

extremities (ek-STREM-i-tees)—the parts of
the body that are the farthest away from the
center of the body; extremities include
hands and feet.

gangrene (GANG-green)—a condition that
occurs when flesh decays

satellite (SAT-uh-lite)—a spacecraft that
circles around Earth; satellites are used to
gather and send information.

visibility (viz-uh-BIL-uh-tee)—the distance
that most people can see clearly

To Learn More

Barnes, Mary A., and Kathleen Duey. *Freaky Facts About Natural Disasters.* New York: Aladdin Paperbacks, 2000.

Meister, Cari. *Blizzards.* Nature's Fury. Minneapolis: Abdo, 1999.

Murphy, Jim. *Blizzard.* New York: Scholastic, 2000.

Oxlade, Chris. *Weather.* Science Fact Files. Austin, Texas: Raintree Steck-Vaughn, 2001.

Rosado, Maria. *Blizzards! And Ice Storms.* Weather Channel. New York: Simon Spotlight, 1999.

Useful Addresses

Canadian Institute for Climate Studies
130 Saunders Annex
University of Victoria
P.O. Box 1700 Sta CSC
Victoria, BC V8W 2Y2
Canada

Federal Emergency Management Association
500 C Street SW
Washington, DC 20472

**National Oceanic and Atmospheric
  Administration**
14th Street and Constitution Avenue NW
Room 6013
Washington, DC 20230

National Weather Service
1325 East-West Highway
Silver Spring, MD 20910

Internet Sites

National Oceanic and Atmospheric Administration
http://www.noaa.gov

National Weather Service
http://www.nws.noaa.gov

The Weather Channel: Encyclopedia
http://www.weather.com/encyclopedia/winter

The Weather Dude
http://www.wxdude.com

Winter Storms
http://www.fema.gov/kids/wntstrm.htm

Index

advisories, 26, 27
air masses, 13, 14
air pressure, 11
Alberta Clipper, 17
Armistice Day Blizzard, 5–7
atmosphere, 11
avalanche, 9, 25

Blizzard of 1888, 29, 31
Blizzard of 1996, 35
Blue Northers, 17

Doppler radar, 25

front, 13, 17
frostbite, 21, 23, 42

gangrene, 21

hypothermia, 22–23, 42

jet stream, 14

lake effect, 14–15

National Weather Service,
    (NWS), 26, 27
nor'easter, 14, 29

ocean, 9, 14, 33

Snowbelt, 17
snowdrift, 7, 9, 27, 31
snowflakes, 13
snowplow, 7, 42
Storm of the Century, 31, 33

traffic accidents, 23, 39
travel, 37

visibility, 8, 27

warnings, 26, 27
watch, 26, 27
wind chill, 19, 21, 27
winter survival kit, 37, 39